W9-CRQ-056

The Blossoming of Belinda

The Blossoming of Belinda

or, Belinda's Ten Terrible Mistakes

Elsie L. Stebbings

VANTAGE PRESS
New York

Illustrated by Tanya Stewart

FIRST EDITION

Published by Vantage Press, Inc.
516 West 34th Street, New York, New York 10001

Manufactured in the United States of America
ISBN: 0-533-13060-3

Library of Congress Catalog Card No.: 98-91126

0 9 8 7 6 5 4 3 2 1

Contents

The Blossoming of Belinda

1
The Flower Gift

It was so unfair! Belinda hated being left at home.
Everyone went out into the big, wonderful world,
except Belinda. She had to spend her days in the
backyard among the chewed-up shrubs and
rhubarb stalks. If it rained she lowered her tail and
dashed into the garage, which was underneath the
house. Fortunately, its back door was always open.

Belinda was a puppy residing in the city of San
Francisco in the sunny state of California. She was
a bouncy, barky, half-grown boxer dog who loved all
creatures and was filled with honesty. Her great
ambition was to be the most perfect puppy in the
world.

Belinda's owners, the Woosters, also known as
Mom, Dad, and Pam (short for Pamela) were
devoted to her. They admired her silky brown fur,
her floppy ears, her velvety black face, and the
white star on her chest. However, they did think
she cried "Yip, yip! Woof, woof! Yap, yap!" much too
often.

On weekdays Mrs. Wooster left home early in

the morning to teach school at Galileo High. Mr. Wooster left for his downtown engineering office. Pam took the school bus to her fourth-grade classroom. No one stayed home but Belinda.

One afternoon, alone in the yard, Belinda felt more sorry for herself than usual. She was tired of tugging up rhubarb. Her soup bone no longer tasted good. Her private dustcloth (really her security blanket) was in shreds.

Then she heard the sound of a motor. The lady next door was arriving home with groceries. For some strange reason, this gave Belinda an idea. Why not dig a hole under the fence and visit this neighbor?

She lost no time in carrying out her excellent plan. Trotting to the fence, she scratched and clawed the ground with energy. Earth and stones showered around her. A damp smell, like a mouse who has been out in a drizzle, ran up her nose. Two astonished earthworms flew into the air. Pansies and petunias from next door came sliding under the fence.

Surprised and pleased with these lovely blossoms, Belinda shook them free of dirt and, making three trips, ran up the back steps to lay them at the kitchen door. She knew that Pam would be delighted with this lovely gift.

Belinda loved to please Pam. In her eyes Pam was the most important and the most beautiful person in the world. Pam was skinny, wore glasses, had freckles and hair that smelled delicious. Also she liked to throw balls for dogs to fetch.

Late that afternoon when Mrs. Wooster and Pam returned home and opened the back door, Belinda, exuberant, scampered up the steps and bounced high with happy expectation. But when Mom and Pam saw the wilting blossoms, they were not filled with joy.

"Wherever did she find these flowers?" Mom exclaimed, her eyes stretched wide with wonder.

Pam picked up the flowers and touched the drying roots.

Then they caught sight of the hole under the fence. They were shocked!

Running down the steps, they examined the hole. Belinda, feeling puzzled, followed them.

Mrs. Wooster shook her head sadly. This was really too much. "We must discipline her," she cried. Seizing the puppy she pushed her face up to the hole and said sternly, "Belinda, this is bad. Bad! Bad! You've been a naughty, naughty dog!"

Dad arrived home just at this moment. He was early. He came clumping down the back steps. "I'm home!" he tooted. Then he saw the large hole under the fence and his face turned red. "What's this?" He glared at Belinda. "When will that crazy dog grow up? Our neighbors will be as mad as wet hens."

Seizing the newspaper he had gathered from

the front porch, he whacked Belinda! She yelped. He gave her another whack. It was frightful! She rushed to Pam for safety.

"Dad, be careful! Not near her face. You could blind her."

Mr. Wooster dropped the paper. They all stood gazing at Belinda's handiwork.

The puppy's brown ears drooped. Her short tail tried to hide between her hind legs.

Mom recovered first from the shock. "I'll apologize to our neighbors right now. We'll buy them new plants."

Pam had an idea. "I know what we can do. We can sink the fence down in the ground so she can't tunnel under."

Dad snorted. "Be reasonable, Pam!"

That evening Belinda skulked in a corner of the kitchen. She felt sorry for herself. She wondered how you can tell which things are sinful. Then she cheered up and ate a big dish of kibble soaked in warm water. This gave her strength. She decided to forgive everyone and try again to be the perfect puppy.

If Belinda had been a flower instead of a puppy, she might have been a dandelion on a lawn, popping up cheerfully each time she was mowed down.

The next day was Saturday. Mr. Wooster rose early, bought chicken wire, and sank it a foot deep in the ground all around the fence. Pam helped him for a while, then she said, "Sorry, Dad—I have to go to basketball." Mounting her bicycle, she rode away.

Belinda watched all this. It was very exciting.

When Dad finished the task at last, his face dribbled with perspiration. "I guess that'll stop the crazy dog," he said, gasping. Upon staggering into the house, he reached the living room and dropped onto the sofa.

Mom revived him with iced tea and a toasted muffin. "See, dear?" she said, "Jelly in all the nooks and crannies."

2

The Supermarket

Saturday morning dawned, twinkling with sunshine. In the backyard, the dew on the spider webs gleamed.

In the kitchen Mrs. Wooster was making out a shopping list. It was a great day to drive to the supermarket and that's what Mrs. Wooster and Pam planned to do.

Mom donned her jacket and hunted for her handbag. Pam added dog food to the shopping list and got coupons out of the kitchen drawer. Belinda, full of excitement, knowing they were going out, jumped here and jumped there. She panted with excitement.

"Can Belinda come?" Pam asked.

"I suppose so," Mom said.

Riding to the market, Belinda perched on the back seat of the car while Mrs. Wooster drove. When they arrived and parked the car, Mom and Pam slid out, closing and locking all doors.

"It's getting hot," Pam said. "We must open the windows a little so Belinda won't get heat stroke."

Mrs. Wooster unlocked the car door. Then she walked off to choose a shopping cart. Pam rolled all the windows down, but not wide enough for Belinda to escape. Then she followed her mother.

Belinda, left out of things as usual, felt rather sorry for herself. She didn't whine or bark—she knew that was wrong. Glumly she watched shoppers come and go.

Then a little boy appeared out of nowhere and started pulling faces at her through the glass.

Belinda was delighted! She wagged her tail in welcome. Whimpering, she pushed her nose through the open part of the window, trying to lick his hand.

The little boy laughed. He danced up and down. "Come out, puppy!" he demanded, turning the door handle. The door opened! Belinda was out in a flash.

She jumped on the little boy and knocked him down. Then she nibbled his ear. He got up and chased her across the parking lot. They ran in front of a bread truck, which shrieked "Toooooooot!" It was great fun.

They saw a large lady loading the trunk of her red car with bags of groceries. All the bags were brown except one white one and the little boy thought that one might contain cookies, which he loved. When the lady turned her back, he couldn't help pulling it out of the cart and running away with it. Belinda chased after him.

They reached a curb and sat down. The little boy opened the top of the bag and turned it upside down. Out rolled lots of sticky sugar doughnuts. They smelled wonderful! Belinda lost no time in gobbling down seven while her companion ate three.

The little boy folded the empty bag, went to a United States mailbox nearby, and dropped it in. He liked to be tidy.

Belinda started to miss Pam and Mrs. Wooster. She didn't want them to get lost or go home without her. She licked the little boy's sticky face to say "Good-bye," and loped back to the car.

No one was there.

She found her way to the store entrance. Peeping through the glass doors, she stared inside. Suddenly the doors swung out and hit her on the nose. She yelped—it was so unfair!

Downcast, she returned to the car. Still no one was there.

Back to the supermarket she pattered. A loaded shopping cart pushed through the door, guided by Mrs. Wooster and Pam.

"Mother, look! Belinda's here!" Pam screamed.

Mrs. Wooster couldn't believe her eyes. "It can't be Belinda!" She gasped.

But it was.

They hurried to their car. Its door hung open as if to say to the whole world, "Enter!"

Shocked, Mrs. Wooster cried, "You didn't close the door."

"Yes, I slammed it, Mom. Really I did."

"Well, you didn't push down the lock."

Pam tried to think. *Did I lock it? Didn't I lock it?* Her thoughts rushed round and round, looking for truth.

"Well, anyway, Belinda isn't lost," Mrs. Wooster said.

Pam hugged the puppy as if she hadn't seen her for ten years. Belinda licked Pam's ear and then her glasses.

Mrs. Wooster started the motor, backed out of the parking space, and carefully drove off.

Was this a perfect ending to the shopping spree?

Not quite. Belinda felt very queer inside. It was as if those seven doughnuts were having a fight in there. Suddenly they all shot out and landed on the car floor.

"Mother! She's sick!" Pam shrieked. "She's just upchucked!"

"Oh, no! Surely not!" Mrs. Wooster threw up her hands and almost had an accident. "We'll have to leave her at home next time."

The puppy scrambled back on the car seat. She wasn't the kind of dog to look wan and wispy, but now she looked wan and wispy. She was so ashamed!

Glancing through the car window, Belinda saw her little friend kindly smiling and waving good-bye. "See ya!" he yelled.

Even this did not cheer Belinda. Her sun had gone behind a cloud. *Will they ever forgive me?* she wondered. *How can I be a perfect Puppy when things go on like this?*

©'99 TREXLE

3
The Huge Dog

Monday morning dawned. After breakfast Belinda was put in the backyard as usual.

At first it wasn't too bad. Coffee and bacon odors floated over the fence from next door. She heard a pan clash, a child laugh, a door bang, a car drive away. A robin flew down and perched on the fence. He sang a song, then floated on his way.

What was there for a dog to do? She couldn't dig under the fence—that was sin. And there was all that wire in the way.

She trotted to the side gate leading to the front of the house and peeped underneath. There was no wire there. By pressing her chin in the dirt, she could see some children's feet tramping by. Car wheels rumbled past.

How great it would be if she could get out into the big, wonderful world without even a leash on her neck!

Sighing, she left the gate and chased a visiting wasp. It was fun for a while. But the wasp had other things to do than play with Belinda. It soon went on its way.

Belinda yawned and sagged to the ground.

Then she saw something exciting. Two ladies next door were unfurling a lawn umbrella—a huge yellow-and-red one as big as a tent. Gazing through a crack in the fence, Belinda saw it rise in the air. It looked scary. Alarmed, she began to bark.

"Quiet!" the neighbor yelled. "Stop that racket!"

But Belinda felt she had to protect the world from this menace. "Yip, yip! Yap, yap! Woof, woof!" She fired an ear-splitting blast.

The ladies endured the uproar for about four minutes. Then, defeated, they lowered their sunshade.

Belinda, feeling she had done a good deed, trotted into the garage, flopped on her blanket, and took a well-earned nap.

Later she woke, roused by a new, teasing scent floating about. Following the smell to the side gate, she peeked under it. Outside stood a giant Saint Bernard dog. Only his feet were really visible, but they were huge, hunky feet. What a playmate he would make! Belinda quivered with excitement and whimpered softly.

The strange dog stooped and sniffed under the gate. For a moment their noses touched. Belinda yelped in delight. Her tail wagged so hard that her whole body shook.

She began to scratch the soil under the gate. She scratched and pawed. There was no wire here. Scratch, scratch—scrape, scrape. The tunnel got bigger and bigger. At last she could get her head under. Good grief! The big, wonderful dog had gone away.

Stiff with shock, she decided she had to find him. Scratch, scratch again. She could almost squeeze under.

Stopping for a moment's rest, Belinda heard familiar sounds—a car entering the driveway, a key turning in the lock of the front door.

Bounding from the gate, she scampered up the back steps to the kitchen door to welcome Mrs. Wooster. She forgot the big dog.

That evening the Woosters spotted the hole under the gate. They cried out in alarm.

"She could have escaped and got lost!"

"She could have been run over by a car!"

"We came home just in time!"

"She's more trouble than she's worth!" Dad bellowed. "A dog like her should live on a farm."

"She'll grow up some day," Mom comforted.

Then Mrs. Wooster got in her car, drove to the tile shop, and bought a large cement tile for Dad to sink under the gate, so Belinda couldn't ever dig under it again.

Meanwhile, Mr. Wooster and Pam had to cook dinner all by themselves.

4

The New Kitten

One weekend, into the Woosters' usually happy home came a confused kitten. This is how it happened.

When Mrs. Wooster answered the telephone, she stood listening a long time. "I'm so sorry!" she said. "How dreadful! Is there a lot of damage? What a brave little mother! Yes, we'll take the orphan, Henry."

She hung up the receiver and spoke to Pam, who was on the sofa, reading. "Your Uncle Henry is bringing us a kitten."

Pam's mouth dropped open. She sat up straight. "A kitten? When?" Her eyes sparkled behind her glasses.

"This afternoon. It's very young. It'll need a lot of care."

Delighted, Pam dropped her book and sprang from the couch. "Belinda," she cried, "you're going to have a playmate. Isn't that neat?"

The puppy, who had been crouched at Pam's

feet, rushed around the room, catching the excitement.

"Is the kitten a boy or a girl?" Pam asked.

"A boy, I think. Uncle calls it Mac. It's a miracle that it's alive. Poor Uncle had a fire in his barn this week. Their cat kept her four kittens in there. When the fire started, she carried one out in her mouth. The barn was blazing when she went in again and brought out another kitten. She rescued a third one, but when she ran in the fourth time, she couldn't come out because the doorway was full of flames."

Pam leaned forward anxiously. "Then what happened?"

"After the fire was put out, Henry and the hired man went in the barn. The air was hot. They found the mother cat near the door. She was curled around her little one, covering him to save him from the cruel blaze. They picked her up. Her fur was singed. She was dead!"

"Oh! No! How dreadful!" Pam blinked to keep tears from trickling onto her cheeks.

Mrs. Wooster hurried on. "Then they saw the kitten was moving—trying to crawl. His mother had saved him after all!"

Pam removed her glasses and rubbed her eyes dry. "Is that the kitten Uncle Henry's bringing us?"

"Yes. Henry has more cats than he needs."

Late that afternoon Belinda barked to announce a visitor. The doorbell rang and Pam raced to open it. Uncle Henry stood there, and in his left hand, he carried a tiny bundle.

When he handed Pam the little black kitten, the puppy could hardly believe her eyes. Was this to be her new playmate?

After they put him down on the kitchen floor, he trembled, crawled feebly, and squeaked.

"He must be hungry," Pam said.

After Uncle Henry left, they warmed milk for little Mac to drink. "Stir egg yolk in it, Mom," advised Pam. "Cat's milk is richer than cow's. That's why we must add the egg yolk. It says so in the puppy book."

"Gracious! You surely will make a good veterinarian," said Mrs. Wooster.

A veterinarian is an animal doctor, and Pam wanted to be one when she grew up. But sometimes she was worried. "The children at school say only boys grow up to be veterinarians," she told her mother.

"You can be whatever you want," Mrs. Wooster said. "You don't need to live your life through a keyhole."

Belinda sat on her haunches with her tongue dangling out, watching the kitten. She saw Pam try to teach him to lap his dinner from the saucer. He wasn't very bright. He bobbed his nose in the milk, sneezing and snuffling. Then he put his paws in it and splashed it on his fur.

At last Mom found an eyedropper and filled it with the milk. He was able to suck his dinner from this quite well.

I don't really need a kitten, the puppy thought. *Though it's nice to have one, I suppose.*

Mr. Wooster came home and stamped into the kitchen. He had been playing golf.

Pam lifted the kitten up for him to see. "Dad, look! Isn't he cute? Uncle Henry brought him."

Mr. Wooster wasn't charmed. "What! Can't he drink from a saucer? He looks like a lot of work. Don't expect me to take care of him."

That evening there was no chase-the-ball games for Belinda. Pam was busy cuddling the new baby. When the puppy sniffed his fur, Pam pushed her away. "He's asleep. Don't bother him."

Hopefully, Belinda brought her ball, but it was no use.

At bedtime Pam found a shoe box and padded it with a white wool sock. She kissed the kitten. "Poor little orphan," she said, as she tucked him in this crib.

Then she put the shoebox on the kitchen floor next to Belinda's large green metal bed with its oval pillow.

Everyone retired for the night.

Next morning the Woosters woke and ambled into their kitchen. They beheld a sad sight. The tiny kitten lay sleeping in the middle of Belinda's big bed. The puppy, too large to get into the kitten's shoe box, lay on the linoleum floor, shivering.

Mom and Pam felt sorry for Belinda, but they couldn't help laughing.

"Why didn't she lift the kitten out and drop him in his shoe box?" Pam asked chuckling.

The puppy saw nothing funny about sleeping on the cold floor. When Mrs. Wooster picked up the kitten, she snuggled down in her own bed and sighed.

Belinda had a friendly nature, but she was disappointed with her new playmate. So much was wrong with him. He was too small. He was too helpless. He was too lovable. She wished Uncle Henry had never brought him at all.

5

The New Name

After school one Monday, Pam rushed home, bringing a friend. The friend was nine years old, had yellow curls, and was eager to see the new kitten.

Belinda, wild with excitement, dashed around the room.

Mrs. Wooster came in from the kitchen, smiling. "Who is this young lady?" she asked.

"This is Flossie Pearl, Mom. She just moved here from Carolina."

"How nice!" said Mrs. Wooster. "Would you like a piece of gingerbread, Flossie Pearl?"

The visitor's eyes lit up. "Yes, please." She staggered to a chair with Belinda trying to lick her face. "I like dogs," she said, gasping.

Mrs. Wooster went to the kitchen and returned with a large, warm piece of gingerbread on a gold-rimmed plate.

Delighted, Flossie Pearl placed it on her lap.

In order to see what was on the plate, Belinda bounced forward and plunked her paws on Flossie

Pearl's lap. Unfortunately, this made the cake slide off the plate onto the carpet where Belinda gobbled it up.

"Belinda! No!" shrieked Pam. "Good grief!" She grabbed the puppy by her collar, shook her, and shut her in the bathroom.

There Belinda, sitting on her haunches, snuffled at the door and pondered. *What had happened?* She had meant to politely pick up the cake and return it to Flossie Pearl. Unfortunately, it had slipped down her throat. Ah! Delicious!

She listened to the voices in the living room. She didn't bark or scratch on the door—she had become a finer dog than that.

Pamela led Flossie Pearl into the kitchen where the little kitten lay sleeping in his shoe box. Flossie Pearl loved him as soon as she saw him. Picking him up gently, she sniffed the top of his head. "He smells like almonds," she said. Then she tickled his tummy. "What are you naming him?"

"Uncle Henry called him Mac."

Flossie Pearl looked shocked. "That's not a good name for a kitten. Not good at all." She tossed her curls.

"What should it be?" asked Pam.

They both stared at the ceiling, thinking hard. They wanted to discover just the right name for a little kitten.

At last Flossie Pearl smiled. "How about 'Jimmy Bob'?"

Pam was delighted. "That's a great name—Jimmy Bob. I like it."

And so it came to pass that Belinda's new playmate was given a name of distinction.

After Flossie Pearl went home, Pam let Belinda come out of the bathroom. The puppy was so glad to be part of the family again that she jumped to kiss Pam, knocking off her glasses. She picked them up for Pam. Then she thought it would be fun to race around the dining room with them, so she did.

"No! No! Stop!" Mrs. Wooster cried. "She'll ruin them!"

But it was so amusing that Belinda couldn't stop. Mrs. Wooster ran to the kitchen, calling, "Cookie! Cookie!"

The puppy never refused food. She rushed after her, dropping the glasses. Pam rescued them and stuck them back on her nose.

"Mom, we're going to call the kitten 'Jimmy Bob.'"

"What a lovely name!" Mrs. Wooster said.

6

The Kitten Grows Up

Mrs. Wooster was glad when Jimmy Bob learned to drink from a dish by himself. Then she didn't have to come home at noontime to feed him. Newborn kittens have to eat every four hours, you know.

Jimmy Bob grew into a sort of imp. He climbed Mom's legs, snagging threads from her hose. He scrambled up the living-room curtains, right to the top. He jumped at the paper roll in the bathroom, tugging down yards and yards. He sharpened his tiny claws on the sofa. He was awakening to life.

On weekdays when they left for school and work, they shut him in the kitchen where he chased his tail "all by his pure little self," as Pam put it. He couldn't get to the living room to nibble the rubber plant, which Pam said might poison him.

Early one morning when the Woosters were fixing breakfast, Pam turned a soft-boiled egg into Belinda's bowl. The puppy was just about to gobble it up when Jimmy Bob bounced into the kitchen and—good grief!—whisked the egg from under the puppy's nose with a lightning paw. It flew up, broke

its skin as it spattered on the refrigerator door, and drooled down. Jimmy Bob lapped up the steaming gold drops.

Belinda gasped! Her egg was gone! She loved her morning egg.

Pam yelled, "Did you see that, Mom? How smart Jimmy Bob is!"

"Yes, he's a genius," agreed Mrs. Wooster, who was pouring hot coffee. She leaned down and tapped the kitten's head gently with one finger. "Being smart doesn't mean stealing, Jimmy Bob. Stealing isn't nice at all."

Belinda hated Jimmy Bob's being so special. Sometimes people seemed to love him more than they loved her.

But she knew that she was fast becoming a fine dog. She no longer got under Mom's feet when she was carrying hot dishes. She no longer barked loudly in the middle of the night when a cat passed by. She no longer cleaned the kitten's dish before he was finished. And she chewed very few shoes.

There was much for a puppy to learn.

7

The French Soufflé

One Sunday afternoon a sharp rain pitter-pattered, then poured and pelted. The Woosters stayed home and felt glum.

Belinda and Jimmy Bob romped up and down in the living room, racing and chasing. Sometimes Jimmy Bob turned a somersault or jumped on a chair for safety. Scampering, round and round they went till the kitten got tired, curled up on the rug, and fell asleep.

The puppy wasn't tired. She nudged Jimmy Bob, pushed him, tossed him. But when Jimmy Bob slept, he slept. With her nose the puppy scooted him roughly across the room.

Pam entered. "Belinda, stop! Let the little fellow sleep."

The puppy's ears drooped. She wondered why she was in the wrong. Why Jimmy Bob wasn't scolded for going to sleep.

A few minutes later, the kitten woke, stretched, went to the front door and meowed. He wanted Pam to take him out for a walk. When she opened the door, he saw the pouring rain and drew back in fright. Then he trotted to the kitchen door. When that was opened, he was surprised and provoked—it was raining out there too!

Mr. Wooster decided to cheer everyone up by cooking one of his special French soufflés. "Find me a big apron," he bellowed.

Mom handed him a pink one with nice ruffles. Tying it on gingerly, he grumbled, "I hope Frank doesn't drop by."

Then came a flurry of flour and sugar, scalded milk, melted butter, eggs cracking.

"Hand me a bigger spoon, Mother. Where's the salt? Beat these, Pam. . . . Now I'll fold in the egg whites."

Jimmy Bob jumped on the kitchen table to watch the proceedings. Mr. Wooster brushed him off.

At last Dad finished the melting and boiling and was spooning the mix into a baking dish. Belinda trotted into the kitchen, shaking an old bedroom slipper. She wanted to show them how high she could toss it, to make them proud of her. The slipper shot up and up in a grand arc and—good grief!—flopped down in Dad's soufflé . . . Plop!

Pam screamed.

Dad gasped, turned scarlet, and shook his fist. "That infernal dog!" He scooped out the slipper, grabbed his big wooden spoon, and rushed after Belinda. Catching her, he whacked her . . . smack! . . . smack! . . . smack!

"Oh, Daddy! Stop! She didn't mean to do it," yelled Pam.

Scared, trembling with fright, Belinda rushed to Pam's bedroom and hid under the bed. A puppy's life wasn't easy!

Soon Pam came into the room, pulled her out, and gave her a big hug. "You didn't mean to be naughty, did you? You're a good slipper-thrower." She tickled Belinda's ears. The puppy snuffled Pam's hair—it smelled sweet.

Mrs. Wooster came into the room and smiled. "Belinda's one of those who make things happen."

The rainy Sunday passed . . . at last.

8

The Drop of Water

Scientists tell us a drop of water is powerful. They say a drop of water—going drip, drip, drip—can wear away a stone.

One Saturday afternoon Belinda learned how important a drop of water can be.

Pam was in the kitchen making hot cocoa for an expected guest. She carried the kettle from the stove to the kitchen counter. At this moment Jimmy Bob sprang at her legs, and she jumped in surprise. The kettle tilted and drops of boiling water fell on the floor.

Then the doorbell rang. Pam ran to the front room to answer it.

While she was gone, Dad came in the kitchen and saw the pool of steaming water on the floor. He was shocked! "Belinda! You know better than this. You scoundrel! Why didn't you ask to go out?"

He grabbed the puppy by the collar, whacked her on the behind, and tossed her out of the back door.

Belinda was upset and confused. What had she

done wrong? Why was she spanked? It was cold and lonely here on the back porch.

Inside Pamela entertained her guest. She served the hot chocolate with coconut cookies and gingersnaps.

Two hours later, after the visitor had left, Pam said, "Where's Belinda?"

"She's been leaking again," growled Mr. Wooster, "so I put her outside."

"Leaking!" Pam was shocked. "She hasn't leaked for months."

"Leaky" had been Belinda's nickname when she was little. But that was in the past.

"Jimmy Bob always goes in his sandbox," said Mom.

Pam nodded. "Yes. He's awfully clean."

Belinda was allowed to creep into the kitchen. They glared at her.

She hunkered down under the table, full of misery.

Yes. A drop of water can wear away a stone, and do other strange things too.

9

Visiting Aunt Mabel

At 9:30 in the morning, the Woosters and Belinda piled into Dad's car. It was Sunday. They were starting out to visit Aunt Mabel, who lived in a nursing home.

Aunt Mabel loved dogs. That's why Belinda was allowed to go. Jimmy Bob had to stay home and mind the house.

After driving along in the sunshine for two hours, they stopped in a little town to lunch at a McDonald's restaurant.

Then they visited a bakery and bought some very special cookies—the kind Aunt Mabel liked. They were called lace cookies. These cookies were thin, full of holes, and looked as if they were made of rich, golden taffy. Unfortunately the bakery only had six left.

Finally they arrived at the nursing home, parked their car, and put a leash on Belinda. They entered the lobby of the large, low building.

Its doors were made of glass. Inside, elderly people sat around in a loose circle to see who came in and who went out. Some people were in wheelchairs and some were taking a nap sitting up—a sort of "sitnap," you might say. There was a faint smell of medicine floating about.

One lady waved at Belinda and smiled. "Come, puppy. Come!"

A gentleman whistled at her and said, "Hi, Butch!"

Someone grumbled. "What's a dog doing in here?"

The Woosters walked down a long brown hall to Aunt Mabel's room and found the door open. There inside was Aunt Mabel, sitting up in bed in a lavender dressing gown with pillows at her back. She was a little lady with white, fluffy hair.

When she saw her visitors, she dropped the book that she was reading and held out her arms. "Ah! Here you are at last!"

Everyone was busy, hugging and being hugged, including Belinda. Mrs. Wooster handed Aunt Mabel the bag of cookies. Aunt Mabel opened it and cried, "Just what I wanted!"

Wriggling with delight, Belinda jumped on the bed. Her keen nose smelled the treats. So Aunt Mabel gave her one. "Now that's all," she said. "These cookies are too special to eat all at once." Then she turned to Pam—"Please have one."

"No, thanks," Pam politely said. She knew there weren't many cookies.

Mr. and Mrs. Wooster also refused, so Aunt Mabel put them carefully away in a drawer in the chest by her bed.

Mr. Wooster asked if her hip was getting better. Aunt Mabel had broken it recently in a fall. "Oh, yes!" she said. "I might even be getting out of here soon."

A wheel chair stood near Aunt Mabel's bed, and Pam asked if she could ride in it.

"Yes, dear. Help yourself. Take yourself for a spin."

Pam sat in the strange chair and pushed it with her hands, turning the wheels. She managed to get it through the doorway, and then she trundled up and down the long halls with Belinda trotting beside her. Doors were on each side of the halls, and some of them were open. Belinda ran inside these, startling the inmates. It was fun!

All too soon the Woosters had to say good-bye to dear Aunt Mabel and start for home.

10

The Mud Bath

On the way back home, they took a short cut along
a narrow road. After a while they came to a motel
that had a field behind it and a small pond. Mr.
Wooster left the road and came to a stop behind the
motel.

"Why are we stopping here?" Pam asked.

"To let the dog run," her father said. "She
hasn't had a chance to relieve herself since we
started. I don't want a mess in the car."

"A good idea," Mom agreed.

Belinda and Pam tumbled out and scampered
into the field. They headed for the small pond—it
looked inviting with plants growing along its rim.

The puppy ran to the edge of the water and
started to bark. She could see a greenish-brownish
frog—or was it a toad?—sitting on a bunch of
floating weeds. Startled by the noise, the frog
jumped into the water and Belinda leaped after it.

The water was shallow, but under it the mud
was deep. In two seconds Belinda sank in mud up
to her neck.

With an effort she struggled out of the sticky, scummy mess smelling awful—like rotten eggs.

For sympathy she rushed to Pam. Pam screamed and shrank away. "No! No!" She held her nose. Belinda bounced up, spattering Pam's glasses with mud. "Down! Down!" Pam shrieked.

They floundered back to the car.

Well! You can imagine what Mr. Wooster said when he saw—and smelled—Belinda.

"What in heaven's name is this?" He clapped his hand to his head. "Rotten mud everywhere!" he roared. "Don't let her in the car. She'll mess everything!"

Mrs. Wooster was shuddering and shaking her head in disbelief. "What a nightmare!"

Pam was rubbing the mud off her glasses.

"We'll have to leave her here," Mr. Wooster bellowed. "And go on without her."

Pam burst into tears. "No, Daddy! No! A Dog's more important than a car."

Mrs. Wooster calmed down first. She even had an idea. "We can take her to that motel." She pointed to the one near the highway. "And give her a shower."

There was silence.

"Absolutely not!" Mr. Wooster thundered. "Motels cost plenty! This mutt will put us in the poorhouse."

Finally, it was decided that Mr. and Mrs.

40

Wooster would drive to the motel and pay for a room. After the manager had gone to the back of his office, Pam would bring Belinda to the room and quickly slip her in. That way the manager wouldn't suffer the shock of seeing her.

That's what they did.

Full of shame, Belinda was glad to get into the shower where no one could see her or smell her but Pam.

Pam scrubbed and scrubbed and scrubbed Belinda. Then she scoured and rubbed and swabbed and sponged and mopped her. At last Belinda was clean and tidy. Her pretty brown fur was glossy again, and the white star on her chest shone brightly.

They all went back to the car.

"Isn't she clean and pretty now, Dad?" Pam asked.

"She'll drive us up the wall!" he mumbled.

Belinda was quiet on the way home. She pondered life's ups and downs. She enjoyed the cool breeze coming through the front window onto her damp fur. There was only one fly in the ointment—she wished she had caught that frog.

11

The Wooden Posts

That particular Tuesday morning was foggy. When Belinda was put out through the back door, she felt its chill. And she felt unwanted—as unwanted as a piece of orange peel.

Several dandelion seeds floated over the fence and nestled in the warm fur on her head. They looked quite ornamental.

She smelled the geraniums from next door and the warm, close odor of the basement as she trotted inside. She heard cars pulling away from houses with people going to work.

She inspected her old soup bone. It was dry and dull. What was there for a dog to do?

She examined the three square posts that stood in a line in the middle of the basement. They were patiently holding the house up, but Belinda didn't know this. She'd seen these posts hundreds of times, but today they appeared to be in the way. She felt like biting one.

She wondered. *Would a very good puppy, a reliable puppy, an admirable puppy chew them up?*

They *did* clutter the basement. Yes. It would be wise to remove them.

Pleased with her decision, she started to gnaw and crunch the nearest one. It felt good. Belinda's milk teeth had fallen out, and her permanent teeth were coming through her gums and were itchy. It was good to give them exercise.

She chewed happily most of the morning until she felt thirsty and went to her water bowl. The water was warm, and there was a fly floating on top. Thirstily she lapped up most of it, including the fly.

Clearing the basement of obstacles was hard work and her tongue was hanging out. She flopped down for a well-earned nap.

Later in the day, she attacked the posts again. She gnawed each one of them. They tasted very much alike.

When Mr. Wooster came home, he put his car in the garage. It was dusky in there. He didn't turn on the light, so he didn't notice Belinda's workmanship.

Next morning Mr. Wooster was in a rush to get to his office on time, so again he failed to notice the altered posts.

Three happy days passed with Belinda enjoying her new project. She crunched away briskly.

Saturday arrived and all the family stayed at

home. After breakfast Pamela saw the front lawn needed watering, so she went into the garage to get the hose. Belinda followed her.

And then Pam's body froze! It froze with shock! She shut her eyes and opened them again, but the terrible sight was still there.

"Aaugh! Eeeek!" she shrieked under her breath. "Good grief! Belinda, how could you?"

Delighted, Belinda wagged her tail and ran to Pam. She thought she was being praised.

Pam threw her arms around the puppy. "Why all this chewing? You terrible little idiot! You dear, dreadful dog! Dad will be furious!"

She started to run up the steps to tell her parents. Then she stopped. How should she break this awful news? How could she shelter Belinda? "Well," she moaned. "I'd better tell them. They'll find out soon enough."

Seconds later Mom and Dad thundered down to the basement.

"Blast her hide!" exploded Dad, on viewing the grim sight. "It's a marvel the house hasn't fallen in!"

"It's unbelievable!" Mom gasped. "She simply couldn't have done all this!"

But she had.

Seizing a broom from a corner, Dad lunged toward Belinda, who cringed in terror. Whack!

Whack! The soft broom went against her sides. She yelped. Whack! Whack!

"No, Dad! No!" Pam screamed. "Unless she's doing it now, she won't know what she's being spanked for."

Mr. Wooster threw the broom in the corner. Fire seemed to shoot from his eyes. "That brute must go! We can't keep her. She's had her last chance. I'll put an ad in the paper tomorrow to give her away. We've had it!"

That evening gloom surrounded the Wooster's dinner table. Mr. Wooster jotted down the costs of repairing the posts on a pad by his plate. Silence hung heavy.

Belinda cowered in a corner, full of misery.

Pamela couldn't eat her dinner—she started to cry. "Dad," she said, "maybe we could wrap chicken wire around the posts to protect them."

Mr. Wooster gave her a bitter glance. He brushed his cowlick from his eyes and went on figuring in silence.

Pamela said, "No thanks" to dessert, though it was ice cream with honey and walnuts on top, and ran to her room.

Only Jimmy Bob was full of good cheer. He toyed with his catnip mouse till the stuffing dribbled out.

12

The Advertisement

Next week an advertisement appeared in the *San Francisco Chronicle* newspaper:

BOXER DOG, free to good home. Tan and white, female, 6 months old, affectionate. AKC registered.

The Woosters waited for results from their ad. Each time the phone rang, the hearts of Pam and Mrs. Wooster beat rapidly. They were afraid that Belinda would be adopted by the wrong people and would not be happy with strangers. Indeed, they were also afraid that she would be adopted by the right people and would have to be leaving them right away.

Pam was upset the most. One day she read about a poor mongrel dog who guarded a lumber yard and was left all alone without food or water on weekends. That night her pillow was wet with tears.

"Mom," she pleaded, "please ask Daddy to let us keep Belinda. He'd listen to *you*."

"I'm unhappy too, dear. But I believe your father's right." She stroked Pamela's hair. "Belinda might be happier living with a family that stays home in the daytime. She's lonely. That's why she gets into mischief."

"But I love Belinda!" Pam threw her arms around her mother. "I can't let her go!"

Mr. Wooster took the leftover chicken wire and covered the basement posts to protect them from further harm.

Pam took Belinda on long walks, fearing each walk might be the last. Her heart ached and felt cold, as if snowflakes were falling on it.

The puppy didn't tug playfully on the leash. She plodded along, feeling her owner's pain.

The next Thursday night the telephone jangled. Mom lifted the receiver. She heard a man's voice. . . . "Is your boxer still available? I raise purebred dogs. I can use her as a breeder in my kennel."

Mrs. Wooster turned pale. She hesitated, clapping her hand to her forehead. "Well . . . but our puppy's used to living in a home—she'd hate being penned in a cage."

"My cages aren't small," said the man.

"But it would be like prison," stuttered Mom. "Belinda enjoys long walks and chasing her ball. Actually I think she'd be happier with a regular family. Thank you just the same." Bang! Down fell the receiver.

Mom stood trembling, appalled at how close Belinda had come to living in a sort of jail.

Friday, after dinner, when the telephone rang, Dad picked up the receiver. "Hello?" He listened a few seconds and his face lit up with a smile. "Gee, Frank, that's great news! We can use a few days at the beach. Thanks a lot, pal. Sorry *you* can't go. . . . We'll start in the morning. . . . Thanks again. Bye."

Dad was jubilant. He loved to fish and his friend Frank had just invited the Woosters to use his seashore cabin for the weekend . . . the long Labor Day weekend.

Pam cheered when she heard the news. "We'll take Belinda," she said. "She's never seen the beach."

Belinda jumped in the air and raced round the room. She was glad to see Pam happy again.

Jimmy Bob watched the excitement, wondering what it was all about. Then he turned a somersault.

Mom's eyes sparkled. "We'll start early, before the birds are up. I'll pack some food."

For the moment the dreadful advertisement was forgotten.

13
The Cabin

Next morning dawned fresh and foggy. When Belinda trotted into the back yard, she found that spiders had embroidered the weeds with webs and the webs were trimmed with dewdrops. She poked her nose in one—it felt cool and tickled.

After breakfast the Woosters got busy. They loaded Dad's big car with food, fishing gear, a pan of sand for Jimmy Bob, Belinda's bed, and lots of other things.

Dad checked the telephone-answering machine to make sure it would record replies to his advertisement to give away Belinda.

Tucking in the last bundle, Mrs. Wooster took a deep breath and said, "We're ready to start."

Mr. and Mrs. Wooster climbed into the front seat. Pam and Belinda settled themselves in the back seat. Jimmy Bob was in a wire cage carrier on the floor near Pam's feet. He yowled—"Meow, meow!" He hated his cage.

The motor roared and they were off.

As they left the city and drove south, they enjoyed lovely views of the Pacific Ocean.

"Maybe we'll see a whale," Pam said happily. "Our teacher says gray whales come down from the Arctic to have their babies where it's warm. Then they swim north again to find good food."

"Meow! Meow!" cried Jimmy Bob.

"I think the whales have all gone north by now," said Mrs. Wooster.

"Meow! Meow!" Jimmy Bob was heartbroken.

Mr. Wooster lost patience: "If he keeps this racket up, we'll toss him out the window!"

But Jimmy Bob believed in free speech. "Meow! Meow!"

Belinda jounced back and forth across Pam's lap. "You're wrinkling my shorts," Pam complained. Her shorts were pink, decorated with yellow daisies.

Belinda pressed her damp nose on the widows. She greeted dogs in other cars: "Yip! Yap! Woof! Woof!"

At last they reached Frank's cabin. It faced the beach and had a path leading down to the sand.

There was sand on the cabin floor, sand in the cupboards, sand on the kitchen table, and sand on the beds. A back window stood open, and that's where the sand blew in.

Mom gave Pam a broom to sweep the floor while she unpacked.

Dad was hungry. He opened cans of little sardines from Norway and made six sandwiches. He poured milk and Pepsi-Cola into paper glasses.

Belinda ate two sardine sandwiches and finished first. Dad ate two sardine sandwiches and finished second. Mom and Pam ate one sardine sandwich each and both of them finished third. Jimmy Bob had no sandwich at all—just a sardine. He played with it until its tail fell off. Then he hid it in Dad's overnight bag, pulling a clean sock over it for safekeeping.

Lunch was a great success.

While Mom and Dad were clearing off the table, Pam said, "I'm going down to the beach with Belinda and Jimmy Bob. They'll love to see the waves."

"Not Jimmy Bob," said Mom. "He's too tiny. He'd get lost in all that sand."

So the kitten stayed home and played hide-and-seek with a lizard that he discovered in a closet.

14

The Beach

Pam and Belinda skipped down the sandy path to the shore. They forgot about the advertisement. Pam, who was barefoot, waded and splashed among the ripples. Belinda, wild with excitement, barked at the waves. She chased them when they rolled out and ran away when they rolled in.

The sunlit beach seemed like a magic ribbon. A salty smell hung in the air. The puppy dug up an old crab shell. Then she discovered a long piece of seaweed and dragged it to Pam. Pam swung it in a circle, and Belinda dodged and chased and jumped over the kelp—it was her skipping rope.

"Belinda," Pam said chuckling, "your legs have grown longer. You're not a fat puppy now. You look like a little fawn."

They wandered along the beach, Belinda scampering ahead.

Noisy seagulls visited them, flying in circles, calling to one another, happy to be alive.

They saw an old man, all by himself, fishing from the shore with a long fishing line. Near his feet stood a pail. Belinda ran up to him in a friendly way and pushed her nose into this bucket to see what was inside. The contents smelled fishy and tasted great.

"Hey, you darn dog! Keep away from my bait!" The fisherman was angry. He took a swipe at Belinda.

Alarmed, she ran back to Pam.

Pam thought the man was unkind until she realized his day would be ruined if his bait was gone.

"I'm sorry, Mister," she said, grabbing Belinda's collar.

The man grunted.

Again Belinda and Pam padded along the beach. There were high cliffs of rock, not far back from the water, and Pam stared at them as they went along.

"Belinda," she said, "let's climb up this cliff. We'll see better. Maybe we can see a whale."

It wasn't easy climbing the peak. It was taller and steeper than they realized. Scrambling, puffing, panting, and slipping, they fought their way up. They zigzagged across the cliff's face. Belinda kept slithering down but tried to stay near Pam. It was hard, hot work.

At last they gained the top. They felt good about this—and what a view! Breathing hard, they could see far out over the wide ocean.

There were plants with fleshy leaves here, stretching out over the edge of the cliff, hiding its rim. It was hard to tell where the top of the cliff ended.

"Whales breathe through holes on top of their heads, Belinda," Pam said. "Isn't that strange? They're called blowholes. . . . Oh! See that steamy spray? Maybe that's a whale!"

Excited, Pam stepped forward. Then she shrieked "Help! Help!" . . . A sharp clatter of stones followed Pam's body as it shot down the cliff, bouncing from rock to rock!

Looking down to see where Pam had gone, Belinda nosed forward onto the treacherous weeds. Then she too was tumbling down, yelping and crashing into jutting crags, pebbles striking her face.

At the bottom the puppy lay still a minute before picking herself up. One of her legs hurt terribly, and so did her head. A warm, salty liquid trickled down her nose.

She limped painfully, searching for Pam.

The girl lay on the ground, partly covered by sand. She seemed to be asleep. Belinda found her and tapped her with a paw, but Pam didn't move or speak.

Sand and gravel continued to slide down the cliff onto Pam. The puppy growled.

She licked Pam's face. It was sandy and salty. Pam's glasses were gone.

Belinda started to bark. She waited, but Pam failed to respond. Then she whimpered—she knew something was terribly wrong. Crouching down, she rested her muzzle on Pam's chest. Her head still hurt and warm drops continued to trickle down her face.

Half an hour passed. The breeze from the ocean turned chill. The sun went behind a cloud. The golden beach turned gray. A seagull screamed wildly as it fled past. Trembling with loneliness and fear, Belinda whined and then howled miserably.

She thought of Mom and Dad back at the cabin. Was Jimmy Bob still playing with his lizard? . . . Suddenly the puppy sprang up! She knew what she must do.

15
Belinda Gets Help

Mom and Dad could help Pam! Belinda just knew it!

Eagerly she started back along the beach. Her steps were painful, but full of hope.

Where she had raced and romped, she limped along. Where the fisherman had guarded his bait, the beach was empty. Where Pam had swung the seaweed, the ocean crept over the sand. The puppy kept near the cliffs to avoid the chilly water.

She struggled and kept going. It was a long, lonely journey.

At last she saw the cabin and the door was open. She barked, and barked again.

Mom appeared at the door and watched the puppy struggle up the path. "Oh, Belinda! Thank goodness, you're back! We thought you were lost. But where's Pam? . . . Pam! Pam! Where are you?"

Jimmy Bob bounced out of the door and batted a bit of seaweed caught in Belinda's collar.

"Dad, come quickly!" called Mom.

Mr. Wooster came from the kitchen where he was peeling carrots. "What now?" he asked.

"Belinda's come home without Pam. She's limping and has a cut over her eye. It's bleeding. Oh, Bill! What's happened?"

Belinda barked and barked. She looked down the beach and barked again.

"She wants us to follow her," said Mom, running down the steps. "Belinda, where's Pam?"

The puppy turned and stumbled along towards the bluff with Mr. and Mrs. Wooster following her.

"Pam! Where are you?" called Mom and Dad, trudging through the sand. "Pam! Pam!" The waves swept in closer. "Pam! Pam!"

When at last Belinda turned aside at the spot where Pamela lay, the Woosters couldn't see their daughter—she was partly behind a large rock and covered with sand.

"Where's the crazy pup going?" Dad asked. His voice was strident with anxiety. "Pam's not *there*."

Belinda was trying to dig the girl out of the sand.

"Come here, you idiot," called Dad. He turned to Mom—"She's actually digging for crabs!"

Mom turned pale. "Look!" she cried, pointing to a part of Pam that the puppy had uncovered. "Pam's pink shorts!"

All in a moment, Mom and Dad were bent over their daughter. Feverishly they brushed sand from her face. Mom was crying, "Pam! Pam, darling! Wake up!"

"She's breathing," said Dad, much relieved.

Belinda stood beside them, eagerly watching and panting.

"Please, Pam! Wake up! Please!" begged Mom.

Did Pam hear her mother? Who can tell? To the joy of everyone, she opened her eyes! Sand clung to her lashes.

"Mom," she said. "Daddy." Slowly she sat up. "Where am I?"

Belinda wagged her tail till her whole body wriggled. She licked Pam's face.

"Stand back!" Dad ordered.

Mom hugged Pam gently. "You're on the beach, dear. Tell us what happened."

"Ouch! My head hurts." Pam pointed to a lump the size of an egg under her hair. "I guess I fell down the cliff."

Mom and Dad stared up in amazement at the craggy peak.

"That would knock out an elephant!" snorted Dad.

"What were you doing up there?" asked Mom.

"Watching for whales."

Pam tried to stand up, but she was dizzy. She almost toppled over. Dad picked her up in his arms, and they all started back along the beach.

"I'm not a baby," Pam protested. "I can walk." But it was no use. Dad carried her anyway.

Belinda hobbled along behind. Her pain didn't hurt so much because she was happy, but she began to feel weak. She lagged farther and farther behind. Soon she couldn't stumble along any more and sank down in the sand to rest a while. She whimpered—they were leaving her.

Pam looked over her father's shoulder. "Where's Belinda?"

Mrs. Wooster turned and saw the small lump lying in the sand. She hurried to the puppy's rescue. "Oh! Belinda!" She gasped. "You poor little thing."

She picked the puppy up, though Belinda had grown quite heavy. Then there were two invalids being carried along the beach.

16

The Hospitals

When they reached the cabin, Dad got out his car and they all drove to the nearest hospital. They went to the emergency room. The doctors found that Pam had no broken bones, but she had lots of bruises.

Because she had been knocked unconscious, the doctors said that she should rest for a few days and come back then if she didn't feel all better.

After that they drove Belinda to a veterinarian's hospital where the animal doctor sewed up the cut on her forehead and put her broken leg in a cast.

At last they all traveled back to the cabin, had a late supper, and went to bed. As the Woosters tucked their daughter in, she said, "Daddy, we can't give Belinda away now till her leg and her head are all better, can we?"

Dad was shocked. "We'll *never* give Belinda away!" he roared. "Without Belinda we couldn't have found you. The tide was coming in. You'd be

63

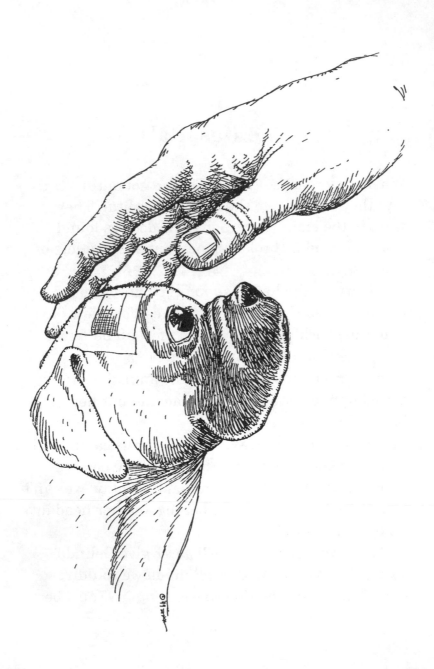

drowned by now! Give Belinda away? Ridiculous! Where did you get that crazy idea?"

Pam sat up. "Oh, Daddy! I love you!" She threw her arms around her father and hugged him. "Belinda's the most wonderful dog in the whole world, isn't she?"

Hearing her name, the puppy limped into the bedroom. Mr. Wooster stroked her head where it wasn't bandaged. Gently he touched the dark velvet of her face. "You're one special dog!" he told her. "You're the most special!"

Belinda basked in this unexpected admiration. But she was very tired. She dropped on the rug and fell asleep.

Next morning, at breakfast time, Mom put down Belinda's bowl, saying, "For the finest puppy in the whole world!"

In her dish Belinda was surprised to see, not kibble, not even her usual soft-boiled egg, but *three* delicious soft-boiled eggs and two pancakes, nicely buttered—one even had a teaspoon of honey on top! In spite of her bandages, Belinda tucked it all away—*slurp, gobble, slurp!*

Jimmy Bob watched her. Unfortunately, he didn't feel well. He upchucked his breakfast.

"I think he's brought up his first hairball," said Mom, thoughtfully, as she rubbed his stomach. "Or maybe that sardine he had yesterday didn't agree with him."

Pam was lying on the couch in the living room, recovering from her bruises.

After eating, Belinda limped in there and flopped down on the carpet near Pam. Jimmy Bob joined them and snuggled into the rug. It was sort of pleasant, all being sick and cozy together.

And so Belinda, this flower of a puppy, blossomed at last. This dog, who lived in the great city of San Francisco in the sunny state of California, had become the most perfect dog in the whole world.